About the Author

Dr Linda Lee-Davies is a well-published, senior, commercial academic who specialises in leadership and cross cultural perspectives for business and university students. During her business and academic career, she has often thought that earlier intervention, embracing difference and diversity, would be even more advantageous for the progression of true and long lasting equality so created the character, Berty Dumbridge as a learning platform for a younger audience. Linda believes that creating a culture of broad tolerance of all difference from an earlier age will form a more equal environment in future domestic and organisational settings.

A Berty Dumbridge Week

Dr Linda Lee-Davies

A Berty Dumbridge Week

Olympia Publishers
London

www.olympiapublishers.com
OLYMPIA PAPERBACK EDITION

Copyright © Dr Linda Lee-Davies 2019

The right of Dr Linda Lee-Davies to be identified as author of this work has been asserted in accordance with sections 77 and 78 of the Copyright, Designs and Patents Act 1988.

All Rights Reserved

No reproduction, copy or transmission of this publication may be made without written permission.
No paragraph of this publication may be reproduced, copied or transmitted save with the written permission of the publisher, or in accordance with the provisions of the Copyright Act 1956 (as amended).

Any person who commits any unauthorised act in relation to this publication may be liable to criminal prosecution and civil claims for damage.

A CIP catalogue record for this title is available from the British Library.

ISBN: 978-1-78830-397-2

This is a work of fiction.
Names, characters, places and incidents originate from the writer's imagination. Any resemblance to actual persons, living or dead, is purely coincidental.

First Published in 2019

Olympia Publishers
60 Cannon Street
London
EC4N 6NP

Printed in Great Britain

Dedication

Linda's dedication
For my fine son, Peter. Always proud of you xx

Sophie's dedication
For Mum, Dad and our Bryony xx

Acknowledgements

Thanks to Sophie Freestone, the talented young artist who has provided the illustrations for Berty and brought him to life just as I pictured him in my imagination.

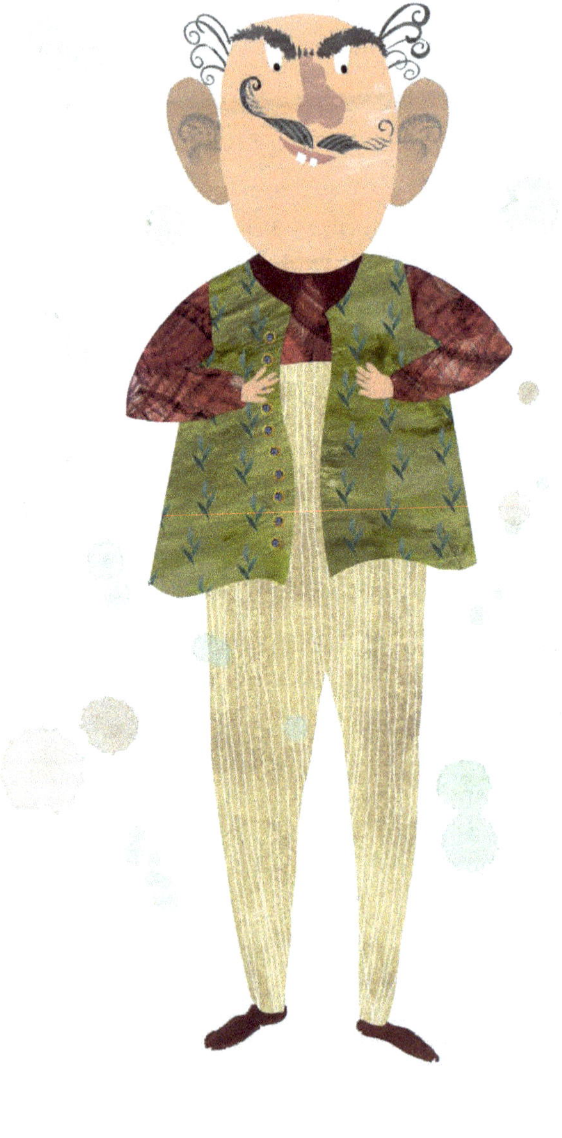

Berty Dumbridge was a very bad man. He thought he was better than other people and often offended them.
- Berty Dumbridge thought men were more important than women. He also thought boys were better than girls.
- He believed white people were better than those of colour.
- He thought being gay was wrong.
- He did not understand disability.
- He mocked those with less money.
- He showed disgust towards transgender people.
- He sneered at other religions.

Berty Dumbridge was wrong but he didn't know it. He needs your help.

Let us travel through a Berty Dumbridge week to see how he discriminates against other people and then you can see where you can help him.

Berty Dumbridge lives in a house in Dumbtown. Berty lives in Dumbtown because even though he is quite old, he is not wise and he is not able to understand equality. Well, not without your help, anyway.

Berty Dumbridge is not very clever so he needs help to understand that men and women are equal. Berty needs help to realise that boys and girls are equal. Indeed, Berty needs to realise that all people are equal regardless of gender, sexual orientation, disability, poverty and religion.

Will you help him?

A BERTY DUMBRIDGE MONDAY

On Monday, Berty Dumbridge got in his van to go to work at his father's tractor plant.

He was wearing his Monday clothes. He wore long trousers. They were light beige and the waist of his trousers reached high up to near his chest. With his light beige trousers, he wore a checked shirt and a body warmer.

Berty is bald on the top of his head with a few bits from the side combed over. He has a funny nose and two front teeth like a rabbit. Monday was cold so Berty put on a warm hat.

The first thing that Berty had to do at work on Monday was go to a board meeting. The meeting was made up of four men and one woman who all had the same level of job and a board position.

Berty Dumbridge sat in his big chair at the head of the meeting and told the woman to go and get coffee for everyone.

The woman, who was called Fairplay Fiona, stood up and said, "Berty, I do not mind getting drinks for my colleagues but I have done it the last three meetings. Would it be possible to share out this task equally to the others?"

What do you think?
Tell Berty Dumbridge what he did wrong.

A BERTY DUMBRIDGE TUESDAY

On Tuesday, Berty Dumbridge got in his van to go to work at his father's tractor plant.

He was wearing his Tuesday clothes. He wore long trousers. They were darker beige than yesterday and the waist of his trousers still reached high up to near his chest. With his darker beige trousers, he wore a plain shirt and a navy jacket with brass buttons.

Berty has a hard, wrinkly face with a very high forehead. He tries to look intelligent even though he is not very clever and only reads one tabloid newspaper. Indeed, he believes everything in the paper and repeats it.

The first thing that Berty had to do at work on Tuesday was go to an operations meeting. The meeting was made up of the same four men and one woman as on Monday. They were there to discuss the new apprentice from the employment centre.

Berty Dumbridge sat in his big chair at the head of the meeting and told the team they had a sixteen-year-old young man starting on the employment scheme. Berty also pointed out that the young man was not white and hinted this meant he would need to be watched more closely.

One of the four men, Diversity Dave, raised his eyebrows in horror and said, "Berty, everyone is equal no matter the colour of their skin." Fairplay Fiona agreed and said that the young man should be treated like any other apprentice. The three remaining men in the meeting stayed silent and made no protest.

What do you think?

Tell Berty Dumbridge what he did wrong.

What do you think about the three men who stayed silent?

A BERTY DUMBRIDGE WEDNESDAY

On Wednesday, Berty Dumbridge got in his van to go to work at his father's tractor plant.

He was wearing his Wednesday clothes. He wore a navy overall as he was going to help on the shop floor with some of the big machinery. He also wore special boots with protection in the toes in case anything dropped on his feet.

Berty has small piggy eyes with big bags underneath. This is because he does not sleep well. He looks older than his age too.

The first thing that Berty had to do at work on Wednesday was go to the plant floor. On the way, he made some bossy gestures to make sure his staff jumped to attention. This served his ego well. "Sweep those leaves off the forecourt now," he shouted to one man.

A tractor had been fitted with a new part and needed to be tested out in the back field. Berty went to oversee the operation. On the way there he overheard one of his staff talking to a colleague, "Last night my son came out and told us he was gay…"

Before the man could finish what he was saying Berty chipped in, "Well, you should send him off to boot camp and get that knocked out of him!" The man replied that he was pleased his son had the faith in him to trust him with such an important thing and that he was really proud of his son. Berty, stayed quiet in a sneering way.

Berty Dumbridge did not understand that he should embrace difference. Perhaps he was scared of it. Berty was also very limited in his views because he did not read much about things and made his mind up on a very small amount of information, whether true or not. As he was not very clever, he could not see the bigger picture properly.

Diversity Dave tried to help by pointing out the modern norm of different families, such as families with two mums or two dads. He also tried to explain how important it was to be open to difference without judgement. Diversity Dave said to Berty, "Being gay is not an illness, it is the way some people are born and it is their choice how to live their lives." Fairplay Fiona stated that such difference should not only be tolerated but that it should also be celebrated and incorporated as a norm. Silent Steve stepped outside of his comfort zone in challenging Berty by nodding in agreement and bravely said, "Live and let live."

What do you think?
   Tell Berty Dumbridge what he did wrong.
   Should you speak up and protect others if you hear someone discriminating against them?

A BERTY DUMBRIDGE THURSDAY

On Thursday, Berty Dumbridge got in his van to go to work at his father's tractor plant.

He was wearing his Thursday clothes. He wore a well-made suit, striped shirt and a club tie. He did not wear it comfortably but it was the dress required for his club lunch. The trousers did not come up as high as his other trousers and his shoes were shiny from a good polish.

Although Berty is not very clever and only got his job through his father's hard work, he likes to pretend he is very important. Berty struts about at his lunch club and tries to fit in with the popular crowd. He does not always understand what they are saying and still thinks that bad comments about other different people will get him liked. In fact, it is the opposite, as successful business people treat difference as a norm and do not make fun of it.

After lunch, Berty had an interview with a candidate for a job at the plant, in the office. The candidate very highly qualified. Indeed, they were more qualified and more technically able than Berty himself. Berty sat in his office with Diversity Dave and Fairplay Fiona and waited for them to arrive.

The candidate arrived on time and carefully made their way over to their seat. Clever Carla had cerebral palsy and took a bit longer to sit down. Her speech was slightly slurred and her body sometimes made random movements she could not always control.

How did Berty Dumbridge cope with this? Well, not very well.

The first thing Berty did was raise his voice and speak slowly as if Clever Carla was not clever at all. He then focused less on her outstanding abilities and more on her disabilities stating, "I suppose we will have to refit the office to accommodate you if we take you on." Fairplay Fiona rectified the matter and stated that it would be very easy to put in a few handrails to help with anything else that was needed and attempted to steer the conversation towards Clever Carla's qualifications and technical ability. Clever Carla had cutting edge experience in new technologies in the industry, particularly with use of 3D printing and augmented reality. No other candidate for the job had this.

Berty Dumbridge did not know what these were as he didn't even use e mail properly.

After Clever Carla had gone, Berty Dumbridge started talking about the other less qualified but able bodied candidates. Fairplay Fiona and Diversity Dave stepped in. They directly challenged Berty and stated they felt that Clever Carla was the best qualified for the job and that simple reasonable adjustments could be made to accommodate the physical disability. They suggested a meeting with the other board members to vote on the matter.

Fairplay Fiona and Diversity Dave addressed the board. Silent Steve now Strong Steve, who had clearly increased his confidence to stand up for what is right, backed the decision that Clever Carla should be recruited on merit. That just left the other two men. Happily, the board voted Clever Carla in and Berty Dumbridge learned a lot from the discussions.

What do you think?

Tell Berty Dumbridge what he did wrong in his interview.

Now praise Berty Dumbridge for allowing democratic discussion and explain why you think the outcome was the right one in the end.

A BERTY DUMBRIDGE FRIDAY

On Friday, Berty Dumbridge got in his van to go to work at his father's tractor plant.

He was wearing his Friday clothes. They were the same as his Monday clothes.

The first thing Berty did on Friday was go to the People Department to sign documents. Fairplay Fiona was the director of the People Department. Fairplay Fiona explained to Berty that all the documents were standard except for one special case. Berty signed the documents in a very important way and sat back to listen to Fairplay Fiona tell him about the special case.

Fairplay Fiona told Berty that a loyal and hardworking member of staff had run onto some financial and home difficulties. Hardworking Harry had been with the company ten years. His wife had become very ill and Hardworking Harry was now the only income in the home as well as having to look after his wife and their three, still quite young, children.

Hardworking Harry asked the People Department whether he could make his full time working hours more flexible through the week to fit in his home responsibilities. This meant he could still earn the same and be at home for his children after school. He also asked if he could apply to the company loan scheme so he could put some equipment in the house to help his wife.

Berty Dumbridge looked annoyed and said – "What is this, a charity?" He went on to moan that if he did it for one member of staff, he would have to do it for all of them.

Fairplay Fiona was angry inside but remained calm and thought about how she would help Berty understand. She took a deep breath and began,

"Berty, Hardworking Harry had been a very good employee for ten years and has often stayed after his hours to help out the company when they were on a deadline – never asking more than his wage. We, as a company, should be there for him now he needs us."

Berty shrugged his shoulders and shifted in his chair.

Fairplay Fiona went on, "Hardworking Harry is not asking for a handout. He has simply asked for an adjustment in working pattern and to secure a company loan which he will pay back. So it will not cost you anything Berty."

Berty Dumbridge now looked more interested.

"Besides," went on Fairplay Fiona, "Helping Hardworking Harry in this way will make you look good to your staff and think about what your club will think of you when you help Hardworking Harry."

Berty Dumbridge was smiling and could see how good he would look so he agreed and signed the document.

What do you think?

Do you think Berty Dumbridge was doing this for the right reasons?

What would you say to Berty?

A BERTY DUMBRIDGE SATURDAY

On Saturday, Berty Dumbridge got up and did not have to go to work.

He was wearing his Saturday clothes. Berty loved his long, high-waisted jeans which had an iron crease on the front and he wore them with a jumper which had a logo on the front.

The first thing Berty did on Saturday, was go into town for a small present as he was going to a black tie dinner party in the evening with two fellow club members and their wives. Berty was going with his wife Horrible Hettie.

Horrible Hettie was horrible to everyone except Berty. She never argued with Berty because he bought her lots of handbags and dresses and she did not have to go to work.

Berty Dumbridge and Horrible Hettie met the other two couples at 7.30pm for dinner. Charity Charlie and his wife Educated Erica and Dynamic Derek and his wife Sensible Sarah.

Educated Erica had just made the time. She smiled at everyone and said, "Good to see you, I just made it, we had an open evening at the university this evening."

Horrible Hettie then said, "Oh, I am so glad I don't have to work. My Berty looks after me." Charity Charlie, who was a big, kind man who raised lots of money for different causes, just raised his eyes to the ceiling and smiled at his lovely Educated Erica. He adored her and knew what was coming next from her quick, bright mind.

Educated Erica calmly looked at Horrible Hettie with a knowing smile and said, "Yes Hettie, I do have to work. I have to work because my brain, my independence, my self-worth and my standing in my own right all require it."

Horrible Hettie did not fully understand the response as she was even less clever than Berty Dumbridge (which was one of the reasons he liked her) but knew she had been dealt with in a clever way.

All six sat down to dinner and chatted away in a lively way about current politics. Dynamic Derek announced they had something special to share with their friends.

Dynamic Derek announced that he was going to transition to being a woman. He had struggled with this for a long time, seen all the right people to help and counsel him and said he would be going ahead with the transition now he is ready. Sensible Sarah would be there to support him as she loved him/her regardless.

Charity Charlie and Educated Erica both stood up and gave Dynamic Derek a big hug. They thanked him for sharing something so special with them and asked if there was anything they could do to help.

Horrible Hettie said nothing. She sat stiffly in her chair with an awkward expression on her face. One part of her was shocked and the other excited that she would have such juicy gossip to share tomorrow when shopping for a new handbag with friends.

Berty Dumbridge laughed out loud, "What do you want to do that for?" he sneered. He continued mocking, "I am not going to be seen with you in a dress!"

Educated Erica stepped in. "Berty, this decision will have been a huge one and we should respect the decision made. We should respect the different needs of others and support how they wish to live their lives. Transgender is a lifestyle choice and right."

Berty Dumbridge did not understand at all and he and Horrible Hettie talked about it all the way home. They made fun of it and laughed at Dynamic Derek.

What do you think?

How would you educate Berty Dumbridge and Horrible Hettie to understand transgender?

A BERTY DUMBRIDGE SUNDAY

On Sunday, Berty Dumbridge gets up a bit later and has a big breakfast at home.

He was wearing his Sunday clothes. They were the same as his Saturday daytime clothes. In fact, they were the same clothes.

Today he had promised his very elderly mother he would go to church. Berty Dumbridge generally went to church at Christmas, Easter, for weddings and funerals. He claimed he was Christian when asked his religion although he was not always kind or Christian in his deeds.

Rocking Rev Richard walked up to the front of the congregation with three others. In his usual happy way, he introduced them.

"Good morning everyone and welcome. I would like to introduce you to Jolly Jeremiah, our local Rabbi at the Jewish synagogue, Kind Kamal, who is leader of our local Mosque and Peaceful Polly, who is the new vicar in the next parish."

Everyone clapped and smiled. Everyone that is except Berty Dumbridge and his mother.

The service concentrated on respecting the religion of others and getting the congregation to think about how they could live and work alongside different beliefs.

Berty Dumbridge and his mother could not get out of the church quickly enough and they moaned all the way as they walked home.

"Whatever next," said the very offensive and discriminating Berty Dumbridge, "We should keep religions separate and I don't think women should be vicars."

Berty and his mother met Educated Erica on the way home. She was walking her dog. Berty proceeded to moan about the service. Educated Erica tried to keep calm as she did not like discrimination of any kind and was very angry inside. She thought it best to try and explain things to Berty in a calm way.

"Berty, we should all respect other religions and try and learn a bit about them. That way we can understand needs at work and beliefs at home so we can blend in together and live and work alongside each other happily. I think it was a great idea to have a service like that. Equality is important. Also women are just as able to be good vicars as men."

Berty looked a bit more thoughtful. He was not clever enough to think of an answer straight away but he did look as if he had learned something.

What do you think?

What would you say to Berty after his horrible comments?

Berty Dumbridge has had a very busy week. Berty has offended many people. They will be very hurt and it is not right to treat people as lesser because of their gender, their race, their sexual orientation, their disability, their financial situation, their gender change or their religion.

If we ever meet a Berty Dumbridge, we should help them do the right thing.

We should respect all difference and treat everyone with kindness as our equal.

Goodbye Berty Dumbridge.

Lightning Source UK Ltd.
Milton Keynes UK
UKHW021003021019
350861UK00006B/50/P